THE PERFECT TRIBUTE

THE
PERFECT TRIBUTE

BY

Mary Raymond Shipman Andrews

Author of "The Counsel Assigned,"
Another Episode in the Life of Lincoln

———

NEW YORK
Charles Scribner's Sons

THE PERFECT TRIBUTE

O N the morning of November 18, 1863, a special train drew out from Washington, carrying a distinguished company. The presence with them of the Marine Band from the Navy Yard spoke a public occasion to come, and among the travellers there were those who might be gathered only for an occasion of importance. There were judges of the Supreme Court of the United States; there were heads of departments; the general - in - chief of the army and his staff; members of the cabinet. In their midst, as they stood about the car before settling for the journey, towered a man sad, pre-

occupied, unassuming; a man awk-
ward and ill-dressed; a man, as he
leaned slouchingly against the wall,
of no grace of look or manner, in
whose haggard face seemed to be the
suffering of the sins of the world.
Abraham Lincoln, President of the
United States, journeyed with his
party to assist at the consecration, the
next day, of the national cemetery
at Gettysburg. The quiet November
landscape slipped past the rattling
train, and the President's deep-set
eyes stared out at it gravely, a bit
listlessly. From time to time he
talked with those who were about
him; from time to time there were
flashes of that quaint wit which is
linked, as his greatness, with his
name, but his mind was to-day dispir-
ited, unhopeful. The weight on his

shoulders seemed pressing more heavily than he had courage to press back against it, the responsibility of one almost a dictator in a wide, war-torn country came near to crushing, at times, the mere human soul and body. There was, moreover, a speech to be made to-morrow to thousands who would expect their President to say something to them worth the listening of a people who were making history; something brilliant, eloquent, strong. The melancholy gaze glittered with a grim smile. He—Abraham Lincoln—the lad bred in a cabin, tutored in rough schools here and there, fighting for, snatching at crumbs of learning that fell from rich tables, struggling to a hard knowledge which well knew its own limitations—it was he of whom this was

expected. He glanced across the car.
Edward Everett sat there, the orator
of the following day, the finished
gentleman, the careful student, the
heir of traditions of learning and
breeding, of scholarly instincts and
resources. The self-made President
gazed at him wistfully. From him
the people might expect and would
get a balanced and polished oration.
For that end he had been born, and
inheritance and opportunity and in-
clination had worked together for
that end's perfection. While Lincoln
had wrested from a scanty schooling
a command of English clear and for-
cible always, but, he feared, rough-
hewn, lacking, he feared, in finish
and in breadth—of what use was it
for such a one to try to fashion a
speech fit to take a place by the side

of Everett's silver sentences? He sighed. Yet the people had a right to the best he could give, and he would give them his best; at least he could see to it that the words were real and were short; at least he would not, so, exhaust their patience. And the work might as well be done now in the leisure of the journey. He put a hand, big, powerful, labor-knotted, into first one sagging pocket and then another, in search of a pencil, and drew out one broken across the end. He glanced about inquiringly—there was nothing to write upon. Across the car the Secretary of State had just opened a package of books and their wrapping of brown paper lay on the floor, torn carelessly in a zig-zag. The President stretched a long arm.

"Mr. Seward, may I have this to do a little writing?" he asked, and the Secretary protested, insisting on finding better material.

But Lincoln, with few words, had his way, and soon the untidy stump of a pencil was at work and the great head, the deep-lined face, bent over Seward's bit of brown paper, the whole man absorbed in his task.

Earnestly, with that "capacity for taking infinite pains" which has been defined as genius, he labored as the hours flew, building together close-fitted word on word, sentence on sentence. As the sculptor must dream the statue prisoned in the marble, as the artist must dream the picture to come from the brilliant unmeaning of his palette, as the musician dreams a song, so he who writes must have a vision of his finished work before he touches, to begin it, a medium more elastic, more vivid, more powerful than any other—words—prismatic bits of humanity, old as the Pharaohs, new as the Arabs of the street, broken, sparkling, alive, from the age-long life of the race. Abraham Lincoln, with the clear thought in his mind of what he would say, found the sentences that came to him colorless, wooden. A wonder flashed over him once or twice of Everett's skill with these symbols which, it seemed to him, were to the Bostonian a key-board facile to make music, to Lincoln tools to do his labor. He put the idea aside, for it hindered him. As he found the sword fitted to his hand he must fight with it; it might be that he, as well as Everett, could say that which

[7]

should go straight from him to his
people, to the nation who struggled
at his back towards a goal. At least
each syllable he said should be chis-
elled from the rock of his sincerity.
So he cut here and there an adjective,
here and there a phrase, baring the
heart of his thought, leaving no rib-
bon or flower of rhetoric to flutter in
the eyes of those with whom he would
be utterly honest. And when he had
done he read the speech and dropped
it from his hand to the floor and
stared again from the window. It was
the best he could do, and it was a failure. So, with the pang of the work-
man who believes his work done
wrong, he lifted and folded the torn
bit of paper and put it in his pocket,
and put aside the thought of it, as
of a bad thing which he might not

better, and turned and talked cheerfully with his friends.

At eleven o'clock on the morning of
the day following, on November 19,
1863, a vast, silent multitude bil-
lowed, like waves of the sea, over
what had been not long before the
battle-field of Gettysburg. There
were wounded soldiers there who had
beaten their way four months before
through a singing fire across these
quiet fields, who had seen the men die
who were buried here; there were
troops, grave and responsible, who
must soon go again into battle; there
were the rank and file of an every-
day American gathering in surging
thousands; and above them all, on
the open-air platform, there were the
leaders of the land, the pilots who to-
day lifted a hand from the wheel of

the ship of state to salute the memory of those gone down in the storm. Most of the men in that group of honor are now passed over to the majority, but their names are not dead in American history—great ghosts who walk still in the annals of their country, their flesh-and-blood faces were turned attentively that bright, still November afternoon towards the orator of the day, whose voice held the audience.

For two hours Everett spoke and the throng listened untired, fascinated by the dignity of his high-bred look and manner almost as much, perhaps, as by the speech which has taken a place in literature. As he had been expected to speak he spoke, of the great battle, of the causes of the war, of the results to come after. It was an oration which missed no shade of expression, no reach of grasp. Yet there were those in the multitude, sympathetic to a unit as it was with the Northern cause, who grew restless when this man who had been crowned with so thick a laurel wreath by Americans spoke of Americans as rebels, of a cause for which honest Americans were giving their lives as a crime. The days were war days, and men's passions were inflamed, yet there were men who listened to Edward Everett who believed that his great speech would have been greater unenforced with bitterness.

As the clear, cultivated voice fell into silence, the mass of people burst into a long storm of applause, for they knew that they had heard an oration which was an event. They clapped and cheered him again and again and again, as good citizens acclaim a man worthy of honor whom they have delighted to honor. At last, as the ex-Governor of Massachusetts, the ex-ambassador to England, the ex-Secretary of State, the ex-Senator of the United States—handsome, distinguished, graceful, sure of voice and of movement—took his seat, a tall, gaunt figure detached itself from the group on the platform and slouched slowly across the open space and stood facing the audience. A stir and a whisper brushed over the field of humanity, as if a breeze had rippled a monstrous bed of poppies. This was the President. A quivering silence settled down and every eye was wide to watch this strange, disappointing appearance, every ear

alert to catch the first sound of his
voice. Suddenly the voice came, in a
queer, squeaking falsetto. The effect
on the audience was irrepressible,
ghastly. After Everett's deep tones,
after the strain of expectancy, this
extraordinary, gaunt apparition, this
high, thin sound from the huge body,
were too much for the American
crowd's sense of humor, always
stronger than its sense of reverence.
A suppressed yet unmistakable titter
caught the throng, ran through it,
and was gone. Yet no one who knew
the President's face could doubt that
he had heard it and had understood.
Calmly enough, after a pause almost
too slight to be recognized, he went
on, and in a dozen words his tones had
gathered volume, he had come to his
power and dignity. There was no

smile now on any face of those who listened. People stopped breathing rather, as if they feared to miss an inflection. A loose-hung figure, six feet four inches high, he towered above them, conscious of and quietly ignoring the bad first impression, unconscious of a charm of personality which reversed that impression within a sentence. That these were his people was his only thought. He had something to say to them; what did it matter about him or his voice?

"Fourscore and seven years ago," spoke the President, "our fathers brought forth on this continent a new nation, conceived in liberty and dedicated to the proposition that all men are created equal. Now we are engaged in a great civil war, testing whether that nation, or any nation, so conceived and so dedicated, can long endure. We are met on a great battle-field of that war. We have come to dedicate a portion of it as a final rest-ing-place for those who here gave their lives that that nation might live. It is altogether fitting and proper that we should do this.

"But in a larger sense we cannot dedicate, we cannot consecrate, we cannot hallow, this ground. The brave men, living and dead, who struggled here, have consecrated it far above our poor power to add or to detract. The world will little note nor long remember what we say here, but it can never forget what they did here. It is for us, the living, rather, to be dedicated here to the unfinished work which they who fought here have thus far so nobly advanced. It is rather for us to be here dedicated to the great task remaining before us —that from these honored dead we take increased devotion to that cause for which they here gave the last full measure of devotion—that we here highly resolve that these dead shall not have died in vain, that this nation, under God, shall have a new birth of freedom, and that government of the people, by the people, for the people shall not perish from the earth."

There was no sound from the silent, vast assembly. The President's large figure stood before them, at first inspired, glorified with the thrill and swing of his words, lapsing slowly in the stillness into lax, ungraceful lines. He stared at them a moment with sad eyes full of gentleness, of resignation, and in the deep quiet they stared at him. Not a hand was lifted in applause. Slowly the big, awkward man slouched back across the platform and sank into his seat, and yet there was no sound of approval, of recognition from the audience; only a long sigh ran like a ripple on an ocean through rank after rank. In Lincoln's heart a throb of pain answered it. His speech had been, as he feared it would be, a failure. As he gazed steadily at these his countrymen who would not give him even a little perfunctory applause for his best effort, he knew that the disappointment of it cut into his soul. And then he was aware that there was music, the choir was singing a dirge; his part was done, and his part had failed.

When the ceremonies were over Everett at once found the President. "Mr. President," he began, "your speech—" but Lincoln had interrupted, flashing a kindly smile down at him, laying a hand on his shoulder.

"We'll manage not to talk about my speech, Mr. Everett," he said. "This isn't the first time I've felt that my dignity ought not to permit me to be a public speaker."

He went on in a few cordial sentences to pay tribute to the orator of the occasion. Everett listened thoughtfully and when the chief had done, "Mr. President," he said simply, "I should be glad if I could flatter myself that I came as near the central idea of the occasion in two hours as you did in two minutes."

But Lincoln shook his head and

laughed and turned to speak to a newcomer with no change of opinion —he was apt to trust his own judgments.

The special train which left Gettysburg immediately after the solemnities on the battle-field cemetery brought the President's party into Washington during the night. There was no rest for the man at the wheel of the nation next day, but rather added work until, at about four in the afternoon, he felt sorely the need of air and went out from the White House alone, for a walk. His mind still ran on the events of the day before—the impressive, quiet multitude, the serene sky of November arched, in the hushed interregnum of the year, between the joy of summer and the war of winter, over those who had gone from earthly war to heavenly joy. The picture was deeply engraved in his memory; it haunted him. And with it came a soreness, a discomfort of mind which had haunted him as well in the hours between— the chagrin of the failure of his speech. During the day he had gently but decisively put aside all reference to it from those about him; he had glanced at the head-lines in the newspapers with a sarcastic smile; the Chief Executive must be flattered, of course; newspaper notices meant nothing. He knew well that he had made many successful speeches; no man of his shrewdness could be ignorant that again and again he had carried an audience by storm; yet he had no high idea of his own speechmaking, and yesterday's affair had shaken his confidence more. He remembered sadly that, even for the President, no hand, no voice had been lifted in applause.

"It must have been pretty poor stuff," he said half aloud; "yet I thought it was a fair little composition. I meant to do well by them."

His long strides had carried him into the outskirts of the city, and suddenly, at a corner, from behind a hedge, a young boy of fifteen years or so came rushing toward him and tripped and stumbled against him, and Lincoln kept him from falling with a quick, vigorous arm. The lad righted himself and tossed back his thick, light hair and stared haughtily, and the President, regarding him, saw that his blue eyes were blind with tears.

"Do you want all of the public highway? Can't a gentleman from the South even walk in the streets without—without—" and the broken sentence ended in a sob.

The anger and the insolence of the lad were nothing to the man who towered above him—to that broad mind this was but a child in trouble. "My boy, the fellow that's interfering with your walking is down inside of you," he said gently, and with that the astonished youngster opened his wet eyes wide and laughed—a choking, childish laugh that pulled at the older man's heart-strings. "That's better, sonny," he said, and patted the slim shoulder. "Now tell me what's wrong with the world. Maybe I might help straighten it."

"Wrong, wrong!" the child raved;

"everything's wrong," and launched into a mad tirade against the government from the President down.

Lincoln listened patiently, and when the lad paused for breath, "Go ahead," he said good-naturedly. "Every little helps."

With that the youngster was silent and drew himself up with stiff dignity, offended yet fascinated; unable to tear himself away from this strange giant who was so insultingly kind under his abuse, who yet inspired him with such a sense of trust and of hope.

"I want a lawyer," he said impulsively, looking up anxiously into the deep-lined face inches above him. "I don't know where to find a lawyer in this horrible city, and I must have one—I can't wait—it may be too late

—I want a lawyer *now*," and once more he was in a fever of excitement.

"What do you want with a lawyer?" Again the calm, friendly tone quieted him.

"I want him to draw a will. My brother is—" he caught his breath with a gasp in a desperate effort for self-control. "They say he's—dying." He finished the sentence with a quiver in his voice, and the brave front and the trembling, childish tone went to the man's heart. "I don't believe it— he can't be dying," the boy talked on, gathering courage. "But anyway, he wants to make a will, and— and I reckon—it may be that he—he must."

"I see," the other answered gravely, and the young, torn soul felt an unreasoning confidence that he had found a friend. "Where is your brother?"

"He's in the prison hospital there—in that big building," he pointed down the street. "He's captain in our army—in the Confederate army. He was wounded at Gettysburg."

"Oh!" The deep-set eyes gazed down at the fresh face, its muscles straining under grief and responsibility, with the gentlest, most fatherly pity. "I think I can manage your job, my boy," he said. "I used to practise law in a small way myself, and I'll be glad to draw the will for you."

The young fellow had whirled him around before he had finished the sentence. "Come," he said. "Don't waste time talking—why didn't you tell me before?" and then he glanced up. He saw the ill-fitting clothes, the crag-like, rough-modelled head, the awk-ward carriage of the man; he was too young to know that what he felt beyond these was greatness. There was a tone of patronage in his voice and in the cock of his aristocratic young head as he spoke. "We can pay you, you know—we're not paupers." He fixed his eyes on Lincoln's face to watch the impression as he added, "My brother is Carter Hampton Blair, of Georgia. I'm Warrington Blair. The Hampton Court Blairs, you know."

"Oh!" said the President.

The lad went on:

"It would have been all right if Nellie hadn't left Washington to-day—my sister, Miss Eleanor Hampton Blair. Carter was better this morning, and so she went with the Senator. She's secretary to Senator Warrington, you know. He's on the Yankee side"—the tone was full of contempt—"but yet he's our cousin, and when he offered Nellie the position she would take it in spite of Carter and me. We were so poor"—the lad's pride was off its guard for the moment, melted in the soothing trust with which this stranger thrilled his soul. It was a relief to him to talk, and the large hand which rested on his shoulder as they walked seemed an assurance that his words were accorded respect and understanding. "Of course, if Nellie had been here she would have known how to get a lawyer, but Carter had a bad turn half an hour ago, and the doctor said he might get better or he might die any minute, and Carter remembered about the money, and got so excited that they said it was hurting him, so I said I'd get a lawyer, and I rushed out, and the first thing I ran against you. I'm afraid I wasn't very polite." The smile on the gaunt face above him was all the answer he needed. "I'm sorry. I apologize. It certainly was good of you to come right back with me." The child's manner was full of the assured graciousness of a high-born gentleman; there was a lovable quality in his very patronage, and the suffering and the sweetness and the pride combined held Lincoln by his sense of humor as well as by his soft heart. "You sha'n't lose anything by it," the youngster went on. "We may be poor, but we have more than plenty to pay you, I'm sure. Nellie

has some jewels, you see—oh, I think
several things yet. Is it very expen-
sive to draw a will?" he asked wistfully.

"No, sonny; it's one of the cheap-
est things a man can do," was the hur-
ried answer, and the child's tone
showed a lighter heart.

"I'm glad of that, for, of course,
Carter wants to leave—to leave as
much as he can. You see, that's what
the will is about—Carter is engaged
to marry Miss Sally Maxfield, and
they would have been married now if
he hadn't been wounded and taken
prisoner. So, of course, like any gentleman that's engaged, he wants to
give her everything that he has.
Hampton Court has to come to me
after Carter, but there's some money
—quite a lot—only we can't get it

now. And that ought to go to Carter's wife, which is what she is—just about—and if he doesn't make a will it won't. It will come to Nellie and me if—if anything should happen to Carter."

"So you're worrying for fear you'll inherit some money?" Lincoln asked meditatively.

"Of course," the boy threw back impatiently. "Of course, it would be a shame if it came to Nellie and me, for we couldn't ever make her take it. We don't need it—I can look after Nellie and myself," he said proudly, with a quick, tossing motion of his fair head that was like the motion of a spirited, thoroughbred horse. They had arrived at the prison. "I can get you through all right. They all know me here," he spoke over his shoulder reassuringly to the President with a friendly glance. Dashing down the corridors in front, he did not see the guards salute the tall figure which followed him; too preoccupied to wonder at the ease of their entrance, he flew along through the big building, and behind him in large strides came his friend.

A young man—almost a boy, too—of twenty-three or twenty-four, his handsome face a white shadow, lay propped against the pillows, watching the door eagerly as they entered.

"Good boy, Warry," he greeted the little fellow; "you've got me a lawyer," and the pale features lighted with a smile of such radiance as seemed incongruous in this gruesome place. He held out his hand to the man who swung toward him, loom-

ing mountainous behind his brother's
slight figure. "Thank you for com-
ing," he said cordially, and in his tone
was the same air of a *grand seigneur*
as in the lad's. Suddenly a spasm of
pain caught him, his head fell into
the pillows, his muscles twisted, his
arm about the neck of the kneeling
boy tightened convulsively. Yet while
the agony still held him he was smil-
ing again with gay courage. "It
nearly blew me away," he whispered,
his voice shaking, but his eyes bright
with amusement. "We'd better get to
work before one of those little breezes
carries me too far. There's pen and
ink on the table, Mr.—my brother did
not tell me your name."

"Your brother and I met informal-
ly," the other answered, setting the
materials in order for writing. "He

charged into me like a young steer," and the boy, out of his deep trouble, laughed delightedly. "My name is Lincoln."

The young officer regarded him. "That's a good name from your standpoint—you are, I take it, a Northerner?"

The deep eyes smiled whimsically. "I'm on that side of the fence. You may call me a Yankee if you'd like."

"There's something about you, Mr. Lincoln," the young Georgian answered gravely, with a kindly and unconscious condescension, "which makes me wish to call you, if I may, a friend."

He had that happy instinct which shapes a sentence to fall on its smoothest surface, and the President, in whom the same instinct was strong, felt a quick comradeship with this enemy who, about to die, saluted him. He put out his great fist swiftly.

"Shake hands," he said. "Friends it is."

" 'Till death us do part,' " said the officer slowly, and smiled, and then threw back his head with a gesture like the boy's. "We must do the will," he said peremptorily.

"Yes, now we'll fix this will business, Captain Blair," the big man answered cheerfully. "When your mind's relieved about your plunder you can rest easier and get well faster."

The sweet, brilliant smile of the Southerner shone out, his arm drew the boy's shoulder closer, and the President, with a pang, knew that his friend knew that he must die.

With direct, condensed question and clear answer the simple will was shortly drawn and the impromptu lawyer rose to take his leave. But the wounded man put out his hand.

"Don't go yet," he pleaded, with the imperious, winning accent which was characteristic of both brothers. The sudden, radiant smile broke again over the face, young, drawn with suffering, prophetic of close death. "I like you," he brought out frankly. "I've never liked a stranger as much in such short order before."

His head, fair as the boy's, lay back on the pillows, locks of hair damp against the whiteness, the blue eyes shone like jewels from the colorless face, a weak arm stretched protectingly about the young brother who pressed against him. There was so much courage, so much helplessness, so much pathos in the picture that the President's great heart throbbed with a desire to comfort them.

"I want to talk to you about that man Lincoln, your namesake," the prisoner's deep, uncertain voice went on, trying pathetically to make conversation which might interest, might hold his guest. The man who stood hesitating controlled a startled movement. "I'm Southern to the core of me, and I believe with my soul in the cause I've fought for, the cause I'm—" he stopped, and his hand caressed the boy's shoulder. "But that President of yours is a remarkable man. He's regarded as a red devil by most of us down home, you know," and he laughed, "but I've admired him all along. He's inspired by prin-

ciple, not by animosity, in this fight;
he's real and he's powerful and"—
he lifted his head impetuously and his
eyes flashed—"and, by Jove, have
you read his speech of yesterday in
the papers?"

Lincoln gave him an odd look.
"No," he said, "I haven't."

"Sit down," Blair commanded.
"Don't grudge a few minutes to a
man in hard luck. I want to tell you
about that speech. You're not so busy
but that you ought to know."

"Well, yes," said Lincoln, "perhaps
I ought." He took out his watch and
made a quick mental calculation. "It's
only a question of going without my
dinner, and the boy is dying," he
thought. "If I can give him a little
pleasure the dinner is a small matter." He spoke again. "It's the sol-

diers who are the busy men, not the
lawyers, nowadays," he said. "I'll be
delighted to spend a half hour with
you, Captain Blair, if I won't tire
you."

"That's good of you," the young
officer said, and a king on his throne
could not have been gracious in a
more lordly yet unconscious way. "By
the way, this great man isn't any re-
lation of yours, is he, Mr. Lincoln?"

"He's a kind of connection—
through my grandfather," Lincoln
acknowledged. "But I know just the
sort of fellow he is—you can say what
you want."

"What I want to say first is this:
that he yesterday made one of the
great speeches of history."

"What?" demanded Lincoln, star-
ing.

"I know what I'm talking about."
The young fellow brought his thin
fist down on the bedclothes. "My
father was a speaker—all my uncles
and my grandfather were speakers.
I've been brought up on oratory. I've
studied and read the best models since
I was a lad in knee-breeches. And
I know a great speech when I see
it. And when Nellie—my sister—
brought in the paper this morning
and read that to me I told her at once
that not six times since history began
has a speech been made which was its
equal. That was before she told me
what the Senator said."

"What did the Senator say?" asked
the quiet man who listened.

"It was Senator Warrington, to
whom my sister is—is acting as secretary." The explanation was distaste-

ful, but he went on, carried past the jog by the interest of his story. "He was at Gettysburg yesterday, with the President's party. He told my sister that the speech so went home to the hearts of all those thousands of people that when it was ended it was as if the whole audience held its breath —there was not a hand lifted to applaud. One might as well applaud the Lord's Prayer—it would have been sacrilege. And they all felt it—down to the lowest. There was a long minute of reverent silence, no sound from all that great throng—it seems to me, an enemy, that it was the most perfect tribute that has ever been paid by any people to any orator."

The boy, lifting his hand from his brother's shoulder to mark the effect of his brother's words, saw with surprise that in the strange lawyer's eyes were tears. But the wounded man did not notice.

"It will live, that speech. Fifty years from now American school-boys will be learning it as part of their education. It is not merely my opinion," he went on. "Warrington says the whole country is ringing with it. And you haven't read it? And your name's Lincoln? Warry, boy, where's the paper Nellie left? I'll read the speech to Mr. Lincoln myself."

The boy had sprung to his feet and across the room, and had lifted a folded newspaper from the table. "Let me read it, Carter—it might tire you."

The giant figure which had crouched, elbows on knees, in the

shadows by the narrow hospital cot,
heaved itself slowly upward till it
loomed at its full height in air. Lincoln turned his face toward the boy
standing under the flickering gas-jet
and reading with soft, sliding in-
flections the words which had for
twenty-four hours been gall and
wormwood to his memory. And as the
sentences slipped from the lad's
mouth, behold, a miracle happened,
for the man who had written them
knew that they were great. He knew
then, as many a lesser one has known,
that out of a little loving-kindness
had come great joy; that he had
wrested with gentleness a blessing
from his enemy.

" 'Fourscore and seven years ago,' "
the fresh voice began, and the face of
the dying man stood out white in the

white pillows, sharp with eagerness, and the face of the President shone as he listened as if to new words. The field of yesterday, the speech, the deep silence which followed it, all were illuminated, as his mind went back, with new meaning. With the realization that the stillness had meant, not indifference, but perhaps, as this generous enemy had said, "The most perfect tribute ever paid by any people to any orator," there came to him a rush of glad strength to bear the burdens of the nation. The boy's tones ended clearly, deliberately:

" 'We here highly resolve that these dead shall not have died in vain, that this nation, under God, shall have a new birth of freedom, and that government of the people, by the people, for the people shall not perish from the earth.' "

There was deep stillness in the hospital ward as there had been stillness on the field of Gettysburg. The soldier's voice broke it. "It's a wonderful speech," he said. "There's nothing finer. Other men have spoken stirring words, for the North and for the South, but never before, I think, with the love of both breathing through them. It is only the greatest who can be a partisan without bitterness, and only such to-day may call himself not Northern or Southern, but American. To feel that your enemy can fight you to death without malice, with charity—it lifts country, it lifts humanity to something worth dying for. They are beautiful, broad words and the sting of war would be drawn if the soul of Lincoln could be breathed into the armies. Do you agree with me?" he demanded abruptly, and Lincoln answered slowly, from a happy heart.

"I believe it is a good speech," he said.

The impetuous Southerner went on: "Of course, it's all wrong from my point of view," and the gentleness of his look made the words charming. "The thought which underlies it is warped, inverted, as I look at it, yet that doesn't alter my admiration of the man and of his words. I'd like to put my hand in his before I die," he said, and the sudden, brilliant, sweet smile lit the transparency of his face like a lamp; "and I'd like to tell him that I know that what we're all fighting for, the best of us, is the right of

our country as it is given us to see it."
He was laboring a bit with the words
now as if he were tired, but he hushed
the boy imperiously. "When a man
gets so close to death's door that he
feels the wind through it from a
larger atmosphere, then the small
things are blown away. The bitterness of the fight has faded for me. I
only feel the love of country, the sat-
isfaction of giving my life for it. The
speech—that speech—has made it
look higher and simpler—your side as
well as ours. I would like to put my
hand in Abraham Lincoln's——"

The clear, deep voice, with its hesi-
tations, its catch of weakness,
stopped short. Convulsively the hand
shot out and caught at the great fin-
gers that hung near him, pulling
the President, with the strength of

agony, to his knees by the cot. The prisoner was writhing in an attack of mortal pain, while he held, unknowing that he held it, the hand of his new friend in a torturing grip. The door of death had opened wide and a stormy wind was carrying the bright, conquered spirit into that larger atmosphere of which he had spoken. Suddenly the struggle ceased, the unconscious head rested in the boy's arms, and the hand of the Southern soldier lay quiet, where he had wished to place it, in the hand of Abraham Lincoln.